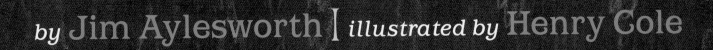

by Jim Aylesworth | illustrated by Henry Cole

NAUGHTY LITTLE MONKEYS

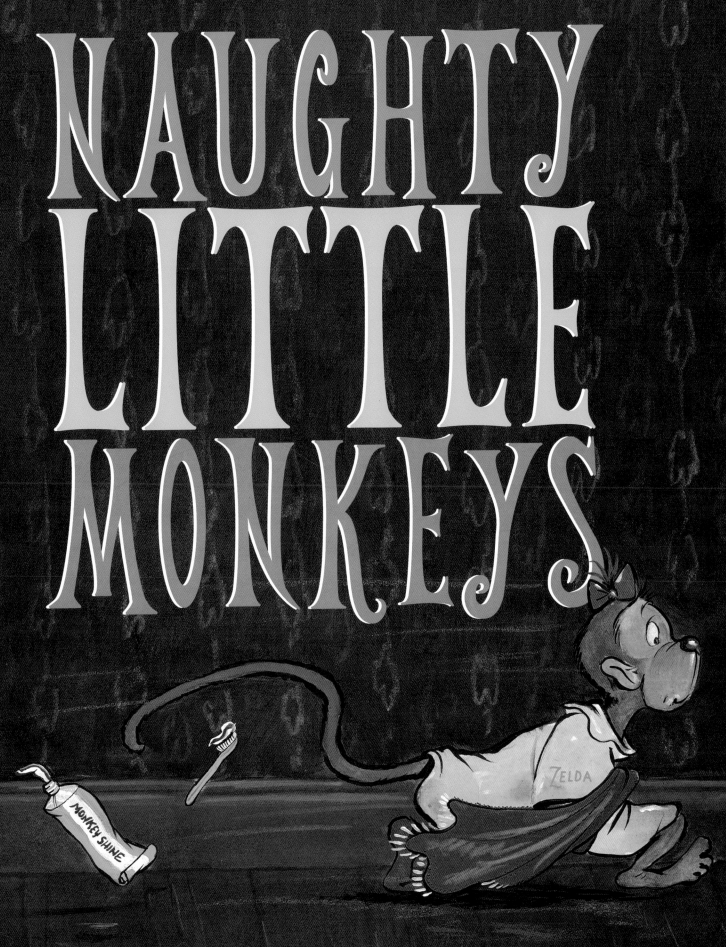

DUTTON CHILDREN'S BOOKS   NEW YORK

To all the naughty little monkeys,
who have so enriched my life,
with love!   —J.A.

To Joan, a naughty monkey if ever
there was one!   —H.C.

Text copyright © 2003 by Jim Aylesworth
Illustrations copyright © 2003 by Henry Cole

Library of Congress Cataloging-in-Publication Data
Aylesworth, Jim.
Naughty little monkeys / by Jim Aylesworth;
illustrated by Henry Cole. —1st ed.
p.   cm.
Summary : Mom thinks all twenty-six of her monkeys are angelic,
but from Andy's wayward airplane to Zelda's trip to the zoo, these little
ones find a way to get into mischief for each letter of the alphabet.
ISBN 0-525-46940-0
(1. Monkeys—Fiction. 2. Behavior—Fiction. 3. Stories in rhyme.
4. Alphabet.) I. Cole, Henry, date. II. Title.
PZ8.3.A95   Nau 2003   (E)—dc21   2002040800

Published in the United States by Dutton Children's Books,
a division of Penguin Young Readers Group
345 Hudson Street, New York, New York 10014
www.penguinputnam.com

Designed by Heather Wood
Manufactured in China / First Edition
10 9 8 7 6 5 4 3 2 1

Naughty little monkeys
Know a lot of tricks,
But Mom thinks they're angelic,
All naughty twenty-six.

 Naughty little monkey
Has a folded **airplane**.
He flies it all around
Until the rest complain.

Naughty little monkey,
Jumping on her **bed**.
It won't be too much longer
Before she bonks her head.

Naughty little monkey,
Eating chocolate **cake**.
If she eats another bite,
She'll get a tummy ache.

Naughty little monkey,
Swinging on the drape.
The curtain rod is bending
Into a funny shape.

Naughty little monkey,
Wearing Mom's **earrings**.
She's been told before
Not to touch her things.

E

Naughty little monkey,
Fooling with the **fish**.
All his fingers in the bowl
Going splashy, splish, splish.

Naughty little monkey,

Playing with her **gum**.

Pulling pink and gooey strings

From her teeth out to her thumb.

Naughty little monkey,
Snipping off his **hair**. . .
But he's clipped too much now—
Off to the barber's chair!

Naughty little monkey,
He's careless with **ice cream**.
The drips are dripping down
In a steady, sticky stream.

I

Naughty little monkey,
She's spreading grape **jelly**.
She's got it smeared all over
Her hands and chin and belly.

J

Naughty little monkey,
Zooming with her **kite**.
The string is getting tangled
On everything in sight.

Naughty little monkey,
Drawing with **lipstick**.
When his mama sees this,
It will make her feel quite sick.

L

Naughty little monkey
Loves his baseball **mitt**.
But playing ball indoors . . .
He really ought to quit!

Naughty little monkey,
Cutting up the **news**.
If Daddy hasn't read it,
He'll surely blow his fuse.

Naughty little monkey,
Waiting by the **oven**.
When the timer starts to ding—
Watch out! There may be shoving.

Naughty little monkey,
Stacking his **pancakes**.
All the syrup's pouring off
Into brown and gluey lakes.

Naughty little monkey,
Underneath his **quilt**.
He'll try to scare his sister
From the fort that he just built.

Naughty little monkey,
Tracking up the **rug**.
Her feet are very muddy
From some holes that she has dug.

Naughty little monkey
Goes speeding down the **slide**.
She is bound to get bruised
From such a wild ride.

S

Naughty little monkey,
Wearing Daddy's **ties**.
He should really know by now
That such a thing's not wise.

Naughty little monkey,
Under Mom's **umbrella**.
It's far too big and heavy
For such a little fella.

V

Naughty little monkey,
With a brand-new **violin**.
By now her brother's patience
Is wearing very thin.

Naughty little monkey,
Splashing soapy **water**.
This way to take a bath
Her mother never taught her.

X

Naughty little monkey,
Banging his **xylophone**.
His mom and dad are wishing
That they had not come home.

Y

Naughty little monkey,
Not careful with his **yo-yo**.
Watch out for that street lamp—
Oops! Now it's an oh-no!

Naughty little monkeys,

Heading for the **zoo**.

That's where all the monkeys go...

When the ABC's are through!